# PINEYWOODS

**Jonathan Watson**
**Pineywoods**



Published by BooxAi
ISBN: 978-965-578-433-6

# PINEYWOODS

## IF THESE WOODS COULD TALK

JONATHAN WATSON

# CONTENTS

CHAPTER 1

# THE TRIP

Where do I begin? Living in a big city can definitely take its toll on you. First, we were taught to grow up and be successful. At least try to be a decent human being and somehow find love and build a family. The good news is I have mine! Caroline is a Southern girl. She's loving, caring and very supportive of her family. She is a veterinarian in the big city who has a passion for animals big or small! Caroline had her son, Michael, while she attended college. Michael was born with a mental disability, and it has been a struggle since Michael was never able to communicate with the world. His mom and him have held it together and it's been them against the world ever since. One day that all changed when I walked into the vet with my dog, Nahla. They have been through a lot and so have I, so it's nice to have someone to call mine. Michael is a very observant, smart, curious young man who has a form of autism that will not allow him to speak. But we got through it! It took him a while to get used to his mom dating again but we made it through that part. We have been together four years now and we still teach each other every day. Some days we find out more than we could ever expect. One thing life has taught me is to expect the unexpected. Now city life always drives us crazy. We needed this trip! So, we thought... Somehow humans think and believe that we are at the top of the food chain. Put yourself in a mountain lion's environment with no weapons and see who comes out on top. Now we were heading out to some fresh air, no neighbors and some peace and quiet. Or so I thought. We didn't realize our lives were about to change dramatically. As the cars passed by Michael listened to his headphones and tapped his fingers on the window. Caroline was reading her book and Jonah was driving in silence thinking about the busy week he had just endured! "Does this place have service?" Caroline wonders. "Did I pack my axe for firewood" Jonah asked her? "I can't keep up with everything, Jonah" Caroline replied.

The buildings turned into fields and the skyscrapers turned into tall pine trees and dense forests that seemed to hold all the answers to the questions we all have soon. As the morning turned into the afternoon they pulled into the mini vacation in the woods and soaked in the pine straws and birds calling in the trees as Caroline jumped out and said, "I have to pee so bad!" "That was a long trip," Jonah replied as he opened the door for her. Michael walked the dog and let her use the restroom as Jonah curiously looked around. Caroline walked out of the house and said, "Michael don't go into the woods!" Jonah said, "Yeah, they have lions, tigers and bears! But, seriously, coyotes, bears and mountain lions!". As Michael glances into the woods from afar, Jonah said, "Who's hungry?". "I'm starving!" Caroline replied, "I could eat a cow!" Michael smiled and walked away with them. The family settled into the winter home and prepared a bite to eat. The wind blew as the woods swayed and the wind howled as the wind chimed sound off. Jonah and Caroline got close to enjoying their getaway from the city as night fell. The next morning Jonah was washing up and Caroline said, "Last night you were a beast," and giggled and said, "I'll start breakfast," as the family sat down to eat. There was a knock on the door.

"Hello, you must be the family from the city. I'm Sheriff Johnson and this is your closest neighbor, Lucas Moore. It's been many moons since this place had visitors and there was some commotion last night. The nearby cattle were slaughtered, and I see you have goats wandering around the property so watch for coyotes or big cats." Lucas said, "Yeah, the bear is getting closer because the land is sold off! Take care folks!" Jonah replied, "We sure will and it's nice to meet you. This is Caroline and Michael and I'm Jonah." The dog barked, Jonah laughed and continued, "That is Nahla! She is a handful!" before laughing. Lucas replied, "I had a dog once and laughed also." Sheriff Johnson smiled and said, "You folks enjoy your getaway and don't get too wild on me and here's my card if you need anything, don't hesitate to call me." The door closed slowly. As they sat and ate, Caroline said, "We should run into town and get a few things, Michael can go with me." Jonah replied, "It's gonna get cold tonight so I'll get things ready here."

CHAPTER 2

# THE ENCOUNTER

Jonah went outside and cut some firewood with Nahla and there was a deer running and she saw it, giving chase into the woods at the blink of an eye as Jonah yelled to Nahla, "Come here!". She turned the corner and ran directly into a wolf and started fighting as Jonah rushed in as he was in shock and grabbed Nahla. But it was too late. The wolf bit into Jonah's hand as he was grabbing Nahla. Jonah was able to get loose and run away from the wolf. He made it back to the cabin with Nahla and sat down on the porch. He grabbed a rag and wrapped it around his hand and took a swig of whiskey for the pain. Caroline and Michael got back from the store, she saw Jonahs's hand and said, "What happened?" Jonah said,

"Nahla ran into the woods and got into a fight with a wolf." Caroline looked in disbelief." There are no wolves out here, just coyotes. The Sheriff said so!"

"I know, but I know what I saw and that was a wolf!" Jonah stressed. "Before I knew it, it bit my hand!" Caroline replied, "You need to go to the hospital! You cannot handle this yourself. That will get infected really fast, and we are too far away from home to have any more problems."

"Yeah, I know," said Jonah, "We came to get away and try to enjoy it. I will go tomorrow, and I will stop and get bullets 'cause you got to be prepared out here."

Jonah just didn't realize the changes he would soon face as his hunger grew stronger every day. Michael walked by Jonah to check on his dad. He had never seen anything like this before and, to be honest, nobody here had. The day turned to night and Jonah washed his hands real good and Caroline helped him rewrap his hand. Michael and Nahla settled down and listened to some relaxing music to settle their nerves. Little did they know things were about to get wild. You see, Michael had a lot to say but time would show that silence was louder than words could ever be.

A father's full-time job is to provide for and to protect his family at all costs. But who would protect everyone else soon? The winter days were short and the cold creeped in like a thief in the night. Michael and Caroline hugged as they looked at Jonah looking down, favoring his hand, still in shock.

## CHAPTER 3
# THE BLACK STONE

The next morning, Caroline said to Jonah, "I saw an antique shop in town on the way to get groceries. These people are not friendly like I thought they would be."

Jonah replied, "Country people stick to themselves, and they know when people aren't from around here. I'm going to build a fire because it's going to get cold tonight and it's the first full moon of the year. Let's start it off right and on a better note!"

The family headed to town to grab some things that might come in handy here shortly. As they arrived, Caroline said, "I'm going to take a look around this shop for antiques and possible bullets."

"Okay. Cool, I will walk next door to the cigar

shop and see if I can find anything good," said Jonah.

Caroline walked in the antique shop and a gentleman greeted her. "Hello, are you looking for anything in particular today or just killing time?"

Caroline whisked around the door as it slammed closed behind her, "I was wondering if you carried Bear spray or know where I can find some?" Unbeknownst to Caroline, the man behind the counter was the gunsmith of the town. His name was O'Rion Hunter. He chuckled and said, "Have you had an encounter or something?"

Caroline turned and looked at him and sternly answered, "My boyfriend got bit by a wolf yesterday." O'Rion responded seriously, "Wolf??!" She looked down at a necklace hanging on the jewelry rack on the counter, "He seemed so sure it was a wolf, and I just knew he must have been super tired or something."

O'Rion looked around nervously and reached his hand down holding a necklace, cleared his throat and said to Caroline, "Take this. Have him wear it. It's a good omen and will protect him. Tell him not to take it off, no matter what! Let's call it good luck." But deep down, he meant that the Black Onyx stone would keep the moon from taking him over.

Looking confused, she replied, "Thanks, I guess. We will need some bullets too."

"You can never have too many of them," O'Rion said and as he handed them to her, he hesitated and said, "Some silver ones wouldn't hurt."

"Thanks for all of your help!" as Caroline reached her hand out.

"O'Rion…"

Caroline shook his hand, "O'Rion, hi, Caroline. Thank you again."

"No problem and if you need anything and I mean ANYTHING, you know where to find me."

Jonah and Caroline met back up and got back to the car where Michael and Nahla were waiting. They headed back to the homestead as the afternoon ended and nighttime fell upon them.

When they were getting settled in for the evening, Caroline showed Jonah the necklace. "I got this when we were in town today. I was told it was for good luck. Maybe you should put it on before you leave the house." Caroline chuckled as she sat on the counter.

An owl could be heard howling in the night and as the thick fog moved in with a crisp wind, the nocturnal animals started to stir. Things were starting to take a turn slowly but surely as Jonah wasn't feeling like himself. A city or town could not contain what was approaching. How many moons had it been? The black onyx stone was a very important piece to the puzzle. Jonah was trying to piece it together, but it could truly be a gift and a curse for sure. No one could truly prepare themselves for the events about to take place. It was supernatural and very unbelievable, to say the least. Michael picked up the necklace and inspected it, then headed to bed.

CHAPTER 4

# IT BEGINS

The family slept as the moon started to climb higher and higher. As Jonah lay asleep, he began to see vivid visions in his dreams. He tossed and turned, over and over, drenched in sweat. The moonlight shined down and beamed through the window down on Jonah. Jonah's eyes suddenly opened, but they were different. They were glowing and non-humanlike. The energy of the moon drew Jonah outside. His senses had suddenly strongly overcome him as he began to jog into the woods that were lit up by the full moon. He heard all the deer running and critters scurrying about as his animal instincts took over.

The next morning, Michael was awoken to the sounds of Nahla barking. He jumped up and looked out his window to find Jonah running into the woods. Michael ran to the back porch and grabbed the lantern and ran after Jonah. He was trying to stay quiet and not crackle the leaves under his feet, so he slowed his pace, slowly walking deeper into the woods. He heard a loud crackle, and it startled him, so he took off running and went around a tree and bumped into Jonah standing there but he was a wolf! Michael was immediately frightened, and he let out a loud scream! He took off running! As he turned around to run from Jonah, he noticed Jonah's boots were torn off of his feet. That's when he realized this wasn't Jonah, this was a demon himself, cursed and damned! He could hear Nahla barking and the goats screaming in the background. Michael was running through the woods as fast as he could with the lantern swaying back and forth out in front of him. He was so terrified and opened his mouth and began to scream! His voice could be heard! Michael was so surprised as he ran into the house and locked the door, ran to his window and looked up to the moon, in disbelief. For the first time, Michael found his voice and in a way no one could imagine. "Was that real?" he thought. He felt as if he had seen the Devil himself! But he knew it was his stepdad! Michael ended up hiding and he fell asleep there until the sun came up the next morning. His eyes opened fast. As he rubbed them, he wished it was all a bad dream. He started yawning and was surprised and jumped when he heard his voice leave his lips. It wasn't a dream at all. He started to remember locking Jonah out. He went into the living room and looked out the front window. He saw Jonah asleep on the porch.

With his stomach turning from Michael's nerves and pure terror from what he had previously seen, he unlocked the door and darted for his bedroom. He began to hear Jonah come in the door, then he heard water running as Jonah washed up. "Hey, Buddy!" Jonah yelled out to Michael, "I hope you got a good night's sleep. I realize there's a lot been going on..." Jonah walked into Michael's doorway drying off his hands, lowered his voice and said, "Let's keep last night our little secret, just for right now." Michael nodded his head, his eyes peeled on Jonah. Jonah knew it would be hard to keep it a secret, that Michael had a voice, but he understood the big problems they could face with unwanted attention. Besides, Jonah had bigger problems to deal with.

Jonah left Michael behind in his bedroom wondering, "How can a man, my own stepdad, turn into something like that and be back to normal again?" Michael had so many questions, but little did he know Jonah had a lot of questions also. Trying to keep this all a secret from Caroline was going to be very difficult, Jonah thought.

"Was that him?" Michael asked himself. "Was that really him? What I saw was a monster!" Michael just could not seem to wrap his head around it. "I need some sleep," Michael whispered under his breath. As he lay down with Nahla as more thoughts filled his head. "Where did Jonah go and how did he get away from it so fast?" He sat in his thoughts until he fell asleep.

Jonah headed into town in search of a bar to get him a cold one and gather his thoughts without worrying Caroline. He found one, went in and walked up to the bar where stood a man in a cowboy hat cleaning a glass out with a towel. "What's going on brother?" he asked to the bartender. "You look like you had a rough night," the bartender chuckled. Jonah laughed and said, "It's that obvious, huh? Let me get a beer!" The bartender slides a bottle over to him, "Here you go… They call me cowboy 'round here. I know it ain't none of my business but what happened to your hand?" Jonah pulled his hand away and tried to act like he was fine. As he hurried and unraveled the bandage, he looked surprised. "I was bit by a..." He stared down at his hand in amazement because he didn't see any marks on his hand. "It's healed up! That is so damn strange!"

Cowboy looked up with a serious look on his face and asked, "You got bit by what?" Jonah still in disbelief said, "This can't be right. It JUST happened!" Cowboy looked at Jonah and said, "How long?". Jonah looked up at him and said, "What?" "How long has it been since you've been bit?" "Two days," Jonah replied without taking his eyes off of his. With a stern voice and a look of concern, Cowboy said, "I've seen this before." Jonah jolted straight up, "REALLY?!" Cowboy stepped towards Jonah, "Really. And before it's too late, I know a lady you must go see." Jonah knew it was probably too late but mumbled, "Ok," with doubt in his voice. Cowboy leaned in close and said, "Go where the river bends and you will find her on a boat." Jonah put his glass down and said, "You don't have a number for her?". "She's not that type of lady. She's off the grid," Cowboy replied as he swiped his money off that bar and tipped his hat to Jonah.

CHAPTER 5

# THE RIVER BENDS

The fog turned across the narrow road and the creatures ran into the night. Goosebumps crawled all over Jonah as he rode shotgun with Caroline and Michael as the streetlights lighted up his bandaged hand. Jonah didn't want to explain to Caroline because he had a feeling she would see soon enough. With the window cracked, he could hear all the animals in the woods near and far. Every light got brighter, and he knew he was running out of time. Michael acted like he was not worried but deep down he knew his stepdad was much more than it appeared. Caroline looked at Michael through the rearview with despair and dreaded as she too felt something was off and had a fear that things might never be the same again.

Streetlights turned to tall pine trees and creepy scenery as the shadows danced with the headlights ahead. As they drove, Jonah told Caroline he was starting to like this place as his demeaner started to change and his senses opened up more and more. Caroline smiled and looked confused at Jonah with a sudden mood change. "That's strange!" Caroline said. Jonah looked ahead without missing a beat and said, "What is?" "Nothing," said Caroline, looking uncomfortable and irritated and left it alone.

The leaves had already fallen, and the bitter cold was setting in. They arrived at the river. Weeping willows danced with the wind. Jonahs's heartbeat raced as he took each step towards the glowing houseboat set off of a long pier that has lots of creeks and crevices. A red light shined into the sparkling water, glowing from a rising moon in the distance. Caroline could sense Jonahs's anxiety and grabbed him by the hand and told him to 'Just breathe'. 'Even she didn't believe me Jonah thought. In a few moments, both would have an idea of how serious this curse truly was. As they approached, they heard a parakeet saying, "Come in!" Caroline and Jonah looked at each other nervously and opened the door.

"I've been expecting you." a lady said. Caroline got startled and looked spooked. "Welcome!" she said. Jonah looked at Caroline then back at the lady and said, "Hello, I'm Jonah and this is Caroline and that's Michael. Cowboy told me to come see you."

"Hi, I'm Lucinda. Cowboy is a knowledgeable man. I am what they call a witch doctor," as she lighted a candle. "Let's step outside to the fire." Lucinda passed a cup of peyote to Jonah. With a confused look on his face, he took a sip and handed it back to Lucinda. Lucinda took the cup back from him, staring at his necklace hanging from his neck. She stopped in her tracks. Hurryingly, she grabbed some sage from her pocket and lighted it. Her eyes rolled back into her head. She began to mumble, "You must leave her and never take that necklace off." Jonah got angry, "But I need to know what to do!" Jonah's voice rose. Lucinda wiped her face with a rag she pulled out of her pocket and said, "You must find what or who did that to you and kill it immediately!" Jonah, with a look of despair said, "That's impossible because that thing could be anywhere by now!" Lucinda replied, "No it will stay close because this is now it's hunting ground."

Nobody had even processed what Lucinda was saying. The clock was ticking with a new moon coming.

## CHAPTER 6
# TIME WILL TELL

Jonah had a long road ahead, but the rest of the family wasn't off the hook yet. Michael hugged his mom and looked at Jonah, hoping he didn't turn back into that thing again tonight. Jonah looked back at Michael and patted him on the shoulder and said, "I got you buddy, don't worry." Michael was not comforted by Jonah's words though knowing what he knew. "Nobody can prepare for this, Caroline," Jonah said, "You don't understand, this is real! That was a wolf and I'm turning as we speak! It's not like the movies. This is a slow process. It takes days leading up to the full moon." Caroline held her head in frustration and worry, "Jonah, we came here to get away! How could this happen?!". "I know, I know babe!" Jonah said as he pulled Caroline in and wrapped his arms around her to comfort her. He looked back to Michael and said, "Put on your headphones for a minute for me Buddy.' Michael listened to him and turned the music up on his phone. Jonah's temper was getting shorter and shorter as he explained to Caroline over and over again the dire need for her to stay there with Michael and stay safe because he was beginning to exhibit new behaviors and unfamiliar triggers. He started tapping repeatedly on the back door like a nervous tick, staring out of it into the night. "You are starting to scare me, Jonah." He turned around real quick and stared at Caroline, "Me, too Caroline! There are no rules or instruction manuals for this!" Caroline stepped towards him and said, "Maybe there is!" Jonah replied, "What they are telling us to do is a little crazy, Caroline."

"I know, Jonah, but she sounded like she knew what she was talking about,"' Caroline said.

"I sure hope so," Jonah replied, "I don't have much of a choice, honestly. What or whoever that thing was that bit me will definitely come back." Jonah looked out the window at the night sky. "Now I feel like I can't leave until I finish this. I can't go back to the city like this or there would be a pitchfork mob after me! You haven't seen it, Caroline! You haven't seen me like that! It's not me anymore when it gets to that point. When it happens, it's like the biggest rush. I can't even explain it. A dark cloud is over our family right now. I can feel the sinister energy in the air." Jonah walked off to build a fire to warm it up inside. He called out to Nahla, but she stayed behind, growling at Jonah. "What's wron…DAMMIT!" Jonah yelled. "I'm sorry, don't be scared you guys!" as he chuckled nervously. Caroline reached down and petted Nahla to soothe her, "It's going to be okay girl, calm down." Nahla kept her eyes on Jonah.

Michael knew how grizzly it was about to get and when it started, all hell was going to break loose. After calling out for Nahla, she came to him and lay down in front of him. Michael lied there staring at the lantern. "It's old," he said, as Nahla turned her head sideways, staring at him because she had never heard him speak before. Her ears perked up as he got up to grab a rag to wipe the lantern down. Michael finished, shook his head and lied back down next to Nahla and drifted off to sleep. The moon grew bigger and brighter. Little did Michael or anyone else know that the lantern was special and was a part of the original curse. It lighted up when a wolf in full transition was near.

The family slept off and on as the lantern blinked faintly on the dresser. Something or someone was close. We just don't know how close, do we? Crickets sung in the night like a choir only they can understand. A howl sounded off like a tornado siren flooding the woods and the entire holler. The nocturnal animals hunkered down. The cougars were even alert because a predator was in the area. An alfa to be exact. Jonah heard the howling and jumped up like the house was on fire, "Is that what bit me?". He climbed out of bed and ran out into the night but forgets his black onyx was missing around his neck. The lantern lighted up brightly and Nahla barked. Michael awoke and sat up in bed. "Who turned that on?" Michael thought as he heard a wolf howl out in the distance. Jonah smelled something familiar in the area as he ran as fast as humanly possible towards the threat. The goats scattered as he ran by and thought, "It that why they come here? For the kill or is it territorial? Mountain lions have a five-mile radius for hunting." He ran up a falling tree across a stream and the howling stopped mid-howl as if it heard him. He saw a deer scurry out of the bushes as something chased it close behind. He watched it jump higher than any mortal man could jump. Growling like a tiger, it snatched the deer mid-jump. They slid off the bank into the water as he ate like Thanksgiving at Grandma's house. "But how?!" Jonah said, "It's not a full moon yet! What's different?" Before he could even move, the wolfman leaped into the woods running away as if he had never seen Jonah. Or did he?

Jonah headed back to the house as he remembered, Caroline and Michael were home sleeping. Unbeknownst to Jonah, Michael was looking out the window, watching Jonah grab his ax by the wood pile and jog toward the house. Jonah walked in and saw Michael standing there with a baseball bat next to Nahla. Caroline was sleeping in the next room. Jonah said to Michael, "Get some rest so you can get your things packed early in the morning. I have to get ya'll out of here ASAP!" Michael said, "Yes, sir!" as he put down the bat. Nahla got in between Michael and Jonah and began to growl. Jonah said, "She's just protecting you, Michael." Michael lay down and said, "I know," and pulled the covers up towards his head. "Lay down and get some rest, I love ya'll."

Jonah fixed a cup of coffee to stayed alert and looked out the window. The coffee was as bitter as this mini vacation turned out to be. Remembering what Lucinda said about killing that thing was all Jonah could think about. He just saw it kill a deer right in front of him. Now Jonah began to get angry because he started to wonder if that thing was trying to be an alpha, was he trying to prove a point? He could feel his neck starting to get warm as he began to feel irritated. Scratching at his neck like a puppy with flees, he breathed on the window and saw his own reflection looking like a distant stranger. Small changes were occurring like his weight increasing overnight. His eyebrows were thicker than before, and his smile was a little more sarcastic. His primal instinct was kicking into overdrive as the full moon approached faster.

Caroline woke up to Jonah standing in a dark corner. He stepped into the light and said, "Good morning, beautiful," to Caroline as she smiled and said it back to him as if she had forgotten the nightmare, they were in. Nahla walked down the hall and stood next to Caroline as if she knew she needed to protect them from Jonah.

## CHAPTER 7

# NAHLA'S REVENGE

*What is a hero? Does it make a person or thing heroic to do what is merely natural? Or is it unnatural to watch nature take its course? How can you judge nature? I don't believe you can, right? Nature is a funny thing that cannot be figured out. Just like the curse inherited by the smallest thing like a decision to take a trip to the country from your safe place that you take, oh, so for granted. The manmade locks and bolts, the change in structure, that's where you find your strength?* Jonah was questioning everything at this point. But one thing was for certain, he had a date with destiny around the corner. No marathon or race, no practice, or no rest, just his dark adversary in his way from his normal life and family now. Being a man and provider was one thing, right? But having to be the hero in a story you were thrown into like a ragdoll with so much precious cargo, your responsibility was on a whole other level.

Jonah made his decision on what to do and how to handle this mess once and for all. Jonah walked to the end of the bed and told Caroline, "Baby we need to talk. I will make some coffee while you get ready then come talk to me. I'll be outside." "Why outside?" Caroline responded. "The goats were in the driveway last night and I heard a ruckus. It worries me so I wanted to go check on them." Caroline started getting ready and replied, "Okay!" Jonah walked outside to inspect what had happened last night. Michael walked out behind him and hugged him. "Hey Buddy, did you sleep ok?" Jonah asked as Michael nodded, "No." Hesitates, "The lantern lit up on its own last night." Jonah – "What?" Michael said, "Yea it was strange. I think it lights up when a wolf is close." Jonah didn't believe him at this point, nothing was a surprise anymore. Jonah thought to himself, "Okay! So, if that's true, that will come in handy." Caroline walked outside with a fresh cup of coffee and sat down. Jonah looked at Caroline and said, "Baby, I need to get you two back home safe. Ya'll need to leave here ASAP. I could hurt the people I love, and I cannot have that. It's way too risky and dangerous." Caroline stood up and cried out, "Jonah! What about you??" "I'll be okay, or I won't, but either way, ya'll will be safe. At this point that's all that matters." He stood up and walked towards the door to go inside. Caroline said, following close behind him, "I can't leave you like this! Michael and I love you and we need you, baby!"." I love ya'll, too, Caroline," Jonah said as he began to get emotional as he started to grab their belongings. "This is just temporary guys." Jonah said as Michael walked into the room. He walked up to Jonah and handed him the lantern and the baseball bat. "Thank you, Buddy!" Jonah said. "You will now be the man of the house while I'm away, ok?" Michael's eyes watered up. "Yes sir," he replied. Jonah hugged them both tightly as if it were the last time. He closed the car door and kissed Caroline one more time as he repeatedly told her they must get going. "Don't stop for anyone or anything." With tears in Carolines eyes, she nodded her head and began to pull off. Suddenly, Nahla jumped out the window and ran back to the house. Jonah said, "It's okay. Leave her with me. I may need her." So, they pulled off, back to the city without Jonah. As they began to disappear in the distance, Jonah kept waving, Nahla now standing beside him like the loyal best friend she always had been.

Ironically, a man's best friend can also be a man's worst enemy. Owning a pet is a great blessing. Having one trust you with their life is a great responsibility. Jonah looked down and says to Nahla, "Welp, it's just us now Sugar Bear! Let's go chop some wood and get a game plan together." When Jonah saw what he saw last night, he took off the necklace and put it in Caroline's bag before she left home. Little did Jonah know Caroline had decided to make a last-minute stop by the antique shop to talk to O'Rion and update the events that had taken place.

The door made a doorbell sound as Caroline and Michael walked inside. "You're back!" O'Rion said. "Unfortunately." she replied, "Jonah is in trouble." O'Rion looked at her with a confused look and said, "Who is Jonah?" Caroline shook her head and replied, "I'm sorry. He's, my boyfriend." "Oh okay, what seems to be the problem?" O'Rion asked. "His wound healed up overnight and the witch doctor said to find the thing that bit him and kill it," Caroline explained. "Hold up, hold up!" O'Rion raised his voice a little, "It healed?" "Yes!" Caroline replied. O'Rion calmed down and asked, "Where is the necklace?". "On him," Caroline said because she was unaware that Jonah had left it with her. She asked O'Rion, "Do you have any more bear spray?? I'd pay you for all the supplies to take to him for me!"." Really?" O'Rion asked. "Yes, I need help bad!" "Sit down," he said. "I need details now." Caroline took a deep breath and started explaining, "Jonah is staying until he can kill what got him in this situation. We are leaving to go home to be safe. I need you to help him find and kill this thing! Can't you help us?" O'Rion knew he had experience with this, and he knew it oh so well. See, he had a secret, but his intentions were good. Caroline said, "Jonah will need anything he can get for his protection and help. I have $300, that's all I have with me." O'Rion began to speak, "It's not about the…" He couldn't finish his sentence before she was shoving the money in his hand and started writing the address down. She hugged him for reassurance and she and Michael walked out the door. O'Rion filled his car with supplies and began the drive out of town.

Jonah was cutting firewood when O'Rion pulled up, except he was not alone. The Sheriff was with him. O'Rion introduced himself to Jonah. "Caroline just left the shop and told me you needed help." Jonah replied, "I need all the help I can get." He handed Jonah the bag of supplies. "Hey Sheriff, good seeing you again," Jonah said as he took the supplies. "Not on these terms." The Sheriff responded. "Can I make you guys some coffee?" Jonah responded, "If I can be honest,"' O'Rion said, "We have been searching for this thing for years. We knew it had to be something crazy like this. There's always been talk about wolves but now proof. Until now. Whatever it is, it's extreme." Jonah turned to O'Rion and said, "These ain't no regular kills we're dealing with. I saw it, but it didn't see me," Jonah said. "See what? When?' O'Rion asked. "Last night, out there in the woods." Orion looked up from the ground and said, "If you've seen him, then he's seen you. Guaranteed." "I thought that might be the case," O'Rion said back. The Sheriff spoke up and said, "Get ready then!" Jonah responded, "I am ready." O'Rion looked at him and said, "No, you're not. It's gonna take God and us to stop this." The Sheriff held his coffee cup up and asked Jonah, "You got more coffee? It's gonna be a long night."

Nahla looked in the distance. Birds flied off as the morning turned into afternoon. Jonah gets the feeling that they know more than they are telling him. He soon found out he was right. Jonah poured them more coffee. O'Rion said, "We've had this problem for ten years. We have tried to get it but could not pinpoint what it was," the Sheriff said. "There have been many rumors around here." O'Rion looked up and said, "It's possible." Jonah said, "What are we gonna do about it? He's very elusive. He can't win this time. It has to stop here. I have to get back to my family ASAP." O'Rion said, "We're gonna figure it out." The Sheriff said, "We don't have much time," Jonah asked, "What about me?" "Jonah, you gather your resources, and we will meet back here in a couple of hours. Meanwhile, I am going to go get more supplies because we need it.'" Jonah and Nahla got ready for what was to come.

The cold winter air was howling through the trees. He grabbed his supplies and the silver bullets off of the mantle. He threw a map down the property that was pinned on the wall. Jonah studied while the fire crackled. Thinking about Caroline's bag and the black onyx stone he put in it, he knew this was going to be bad. No control, no reasoning and no conscious decision. Just carnage.

Jonah saw headlights coming down the drive. It was the Sheriff and O'Rion. He spotlighted the woods, pulling up to the house. Nahla stood alert and silent. That was her strong point. She would never leave Jonah's side at the end of the day. "The sun's falling fast. Let's unload these supplies and start planning," the Sheriff said. "We have a tree stand, bear spray, some log chains and more ammo," O'Rion said to them. "I will have a fire ready," Jonah said. They came up with a hopeful plan to reverse the curse once and for all. Sheriff Johnson said, "I've been working for the department for fifteen years. I spent four years in Afghanistan as a door gunner." "Well, you must be handy with the guns then," Jonah said. "I suppose," Sheriff replied. O'Rion said, "I'm twenty years strong as a gunsmith and a survivalist trainer in the wildlife refuge." Sheriff said, "We developed a good relationship from all the nuisance calls we got." Jonah said, "I milled lumbar and cut trees for twenty years. Before this I was a mechanic for a couple of years. I hurt my foot and had to slow down. The moon is rising fast. We have to get going."

"Door gunner, set up the tree stand," Orion said. Jonah replied, "Come on, I'll show you where we need it." O'Rion loaded the guns and started setting a bear trap and a string with a bell from the antique shop. He had a lot of relics he had obtained through the years. O'Rion said, "We're also equipped with wolves Bain, a powerful plant. It takes its strength away." Jonah and the Sheriff finished setting up the tree stand. Jonah looked through binoculars at the house. "Let's gather a lot of wood to keep it well lit. We don't need any surprises," the Sheriff said. "I agree," Jonah replied. He slammed the axe into a big log until it split. "I'm going to do that to his head when I get the chance!" Jonah yelled out in anger. O'Rion walked over to Jonah and said, "Let's stay calm. What are you going to do if you change? We brought them chains and Sheriff Johnson has silver handcuffs. We can secure you in the barn until we know you don't turn." "I understand," Jonah said. "I think that's our safest bet. Well let's get these traps before it gets too late," said Sheriff Johnson. They set traps along the wood line with wire and wooden spikes that cut like spears.

Nahla lay low and watched them work as she stayed alert and stood guard for them. The lantern on the porch began to flicker and caught Nahla's attention. She began to bark as she watched them set up the chains in the barn. "I have a good idea," said O'Rion. "Let's grab the goats as bait and lead him to the traps." "Great Idea brother," said Sheriff Johnson. "Let's get going guys." They all got ready to head to the barn and Nahla began to alert them by growling and barking. It was getting close. They knew it. Jonah said, "Sheriff, take a goat by your tree stand and tie it to a tree so you have a clear shot. O'Rion, get me tied up in the barn. Nahla, come." O'Rion grabbed the bag of chains and locked and headed to the barn with them. "I hate I have to tie you up brother," O'Rion said to Jonah. "I understand we have to do this. I don't like it either. I just appreciate you helping me and fighting for my family," Jonah said. "No worries," O'Rion said. "I gotta tell you something, Jonah. I got bit 15 years ago and I want him too! This is personal..." "So, you're a…" Jonah said quickly. "Shhhh!" O'Rion replied, "I got your back. I have my necklace with me," O'Rion said. "So, you can change too?" Jonah asked O'Rion. "Yes, but I can control it," O'Rion said as he looked up at Jonah as Jonah watches O'Rion's eyes begin to glow! "Damn, come and get me if I don't change. If I do, you'll know it!" Jonah said as O'Rion finished chaining him up.

Sheriff got prepared for the wolf as he went to his location of surprise where the deer blinds were set up. Walking slowly, Sheriff Johnson heard the animals in the woods scatter as if they knew the wolf was there. Sheriff Johnson began to spray deer urine on him for the scent, put his rifle on a strap around his neck and got into position up in the tree stand. The wind blew and carried the scent downstream of the creek below.

Nahla got up to the barn and waited and watched Jonah like she knew why he was chained up. Jonah looked up at her and smiled, "Thank you for protecting me, baby. I love you with all of my heart and soul. I miss Caroline and Michael. I pray we make it home." Nahla lay down with only her eyes visible like she felt the energy changing in the air. O'Rion took the other goat outside the barn down by the fire so he could be seen. O'Rion then set a trap wire with a bell by the wood line. An owl sounded off and flew away and the lantern started to glow. Sure enough, the clouds moved, and the moon was full once again. Michael whispered up to Nahla, "Watch out and stay put girl!" She watched the door. O'Rion lay down in a ditch in the yard after he put another log on the fire and stoked it. He was in the dark with a rifle as well and bear spray. He could take his necklace off, but he wouldn't have control. He heard a howl in the distance as Nahla rose up on guard. "Lay down," Jonah said to Nahla, as Jonah began to sweat. O'Rion took aim toward the woods, skimming around. Sheriff Johnson surveyed the area with night vision goggles. He said to his self, "I knew these would come in handy." He looked around and saw a grown mountain lion about to charge him up the tree. All of a sudden, the wolfman leaped out of the darkness, grabbed the lion and snapped his neck. "My God!" Sheriff mumbled as he tried to get eyes on the wolf again. He saw him running towards the property and fired a shot. Jonah looked in that direction and began to get angry. O'Rion heard the shot and ran for the tree line. The wolf saw the goat the lion was watching and ran in that direction. Sheriff Johnson fired a shot again and the wolf suddenly stopped, turned and looked at him. He fired again and missed. The wolfman swiped the Sheriff like a rag doll and knocked him down into a stream. The wolfman ran into the woods. Nahla looked at Jonah as he bended over and looked back up as he was changing into a wolf himself. Nahla lay down as O'Rion set another fire closer to the barn so they could see. The wire tripped at the wood line and the bell rings closed by. He finally saw the wolfman running across the yard, stood up and fired, hitting the wolfman in the shoulder. It just angered the wolf as he ran towards O'Rion. He fired again as the wolfman tackled him and knocked him into a ditch. The Sheriff wasn't doing well at all as he tried to get out of the water from the stream. Guided by the light from the fire, he crawled out of the stream towards it. A loud noise out of nowhere, Jonah jumped out of the barn as a wolf and tackled the Alpha wolfman. The Alpha swiped Jonah with ease, and he flew backwards. O'Rion came to and found his gun and fired another shot, distracting the wolfman for a split second. Jonah swiped him across the neck, and they started to tumble down the hill fighting. The moon lit up the sky. The fire was a beacon of disaster. O'Rion shot again and hit the wolfman in the chest. Jonah leaped across the fire and swung on the wolfman and missed. It was a real battle.

With Jonah laying down, in need, O'Rion looked for more bullets as the wolfman had the upper hand on Jonah. O'Rion whistled at the wolfman and shot him. Nahla jumped across the yard, hit the wolfman in the chest and pushed him into the fire. Jonah mustarded up the strength to get up and went towards Nahla to check on her. The wolfman jumped back out of the fire and Jonah swiped his head off with his sharp claws. Within moments, the wolfman began to turn back into human form. It was Lucas, the neighbor! O'Rion called Nahla and they lay down on the ground and watched because they knew it was not over yet. Jonah lay down and started slowly turning back into a very wounded, mortal man. "She saved me," Jonah said into the night as he could barely talk. "She sure did," O'Rion replied. "Where is the Sheriff at?" Jonah asked. "I don't know," O'Rion said. Suddenly Sheriff Johnson was heard yelling for help from a distance. Nahla ran to check on him and started licking his face. O'Rion helped him stay still.

They called for help. Within thirty minutes, red lights lighted up the forest. Only they knew what truly happened that night. Jonah was happy to be alive as he began to think about his family. "It's not done," Jonah said to O'Rion, "You're still the same so I need to help you like you helped me, and I must return the favor." "That's another battle my friend," said O'Rion. "No," Jonah replied, "We are family now. Let's go home girl," Jonah said to Nahla. O'Rion said, "I'll take you home." They left out to the city down the old gravel road, leaving all the secrets in the trees. Jonah stared out the window at the woods and said, "I'll be back though."

The End.

Author Jonathan Watson

Special Thanks to Contributors:

Corrinna Hartman

Tony Dupot

Kevin Bernard, Stack Up or Shut Up, LLC

Okorie Mass, Mass Home Improvement, LLC

~ This book is dedicated to my loving sister, Heather Watson. We love and miss you. ~

Printed in the USA
CPSIA information can be obtained
at www.ICGtesting.com
LVHW041132131023
760673LV00044B/823